Betsy Everitt

Harcourt Brace Jovanovich, Publishers

San Diego   New York   London

HBJ

Requests for permission to make copies of any part
of the work should be mailed to: Permissions Department,
Harcourt Brace Jovanovich, Publishers, 8th Floor, Orlando, Florida 32887.

Library of Congress Cataloging-in-Publication Data
Everitt, Betsy.
Mean soup/Betsy Everitt. — 1st ed.
p.   cm.
Summary: Horace feels really mean at the end of a bad day
until he helps his mother make Mean Soup.
ISBN 0-15-253146-7
[1. Anger — Fiction. 2. Cookery — Fiction.] I. Title.
PZ7.E9217Me   1992
[E] — dc20   91-15244

First edition   A B C D E

The paintings in this book were done in gouache on watercolor paper.
The text and display type were set in Century Expanded
by Thompson Type, San Diego, California.
Color separations were made by Bright Arts, Ltd., Hong Kong.
Printed and bound by Tien Wah Press, Singapore
Production supervision by Warren Wallerstein and Ginger Boyer
Designed by Camilla Filancia

For Tim, Matt, and Pete

It had been a bad day for Horace.

He forgot the answer to question three.

Zelda gave him a love note.

And Lulu, the show-and-tell cow, stepped on his foot.

As if this wasn't enough, his mother sent
Miss Pearl to pick him up from school.

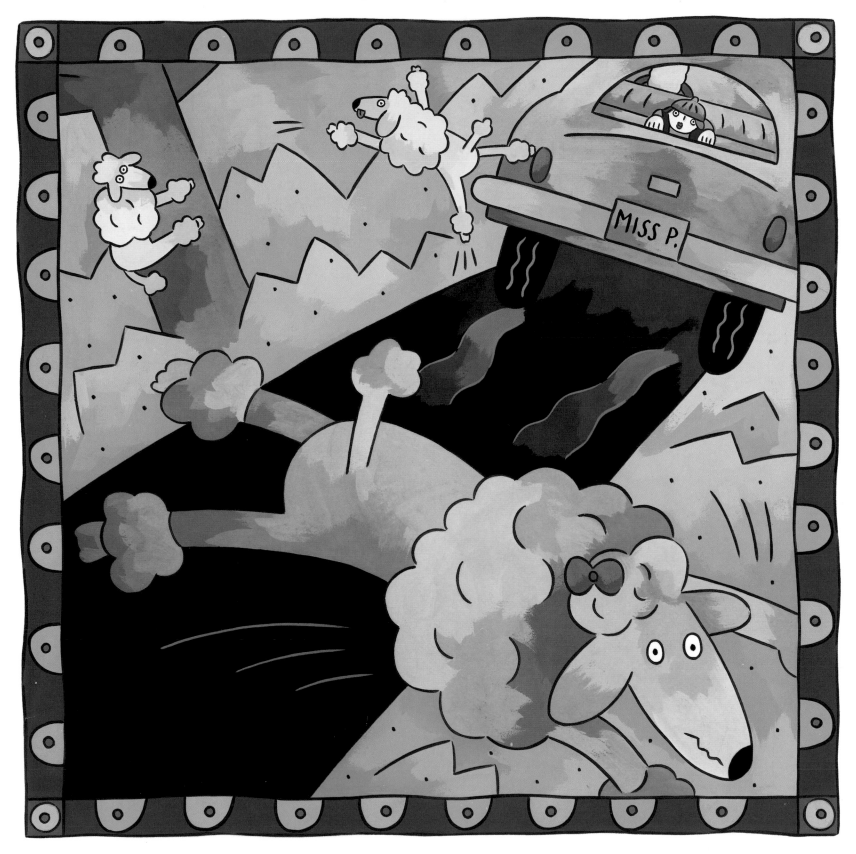

She swerved and screeched and nearly killed
three poodles before they made it home.

Horace felt so mean he stepped on a flower.

His mother said, "Hello." And Horace hissed.

His mother said, "How was your day?"
And Horace growled.

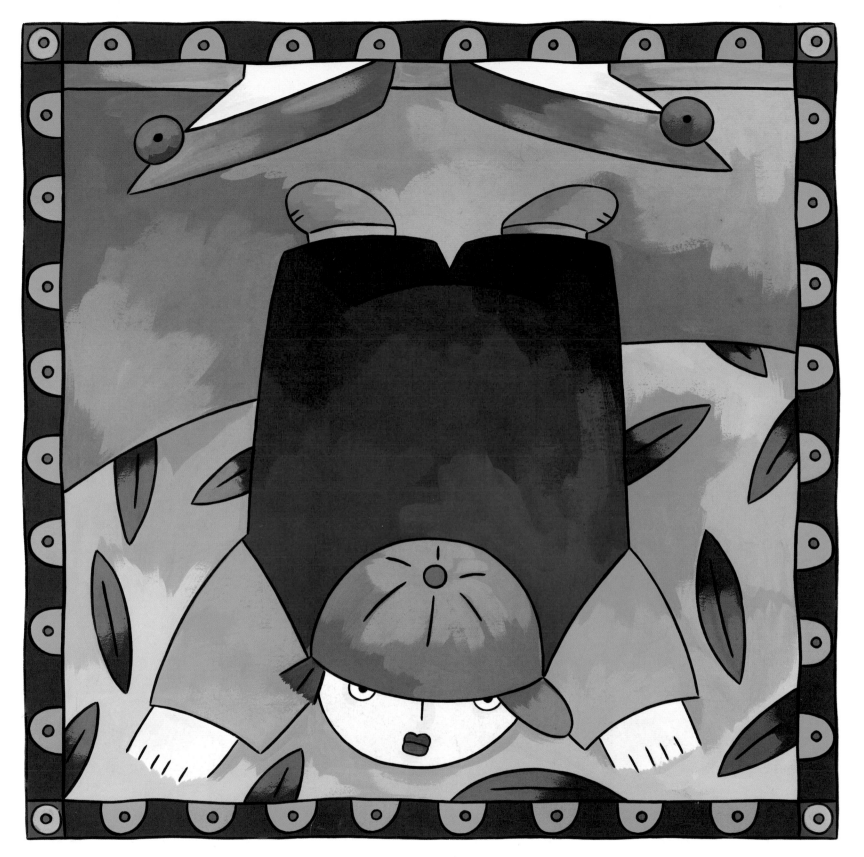

His mother said, "Did you thank Miss Pearl?"
And Horace fell on the floor.

"Let's make soup!" his mother said.

Horace lay still. He felt mean.
And he *wasn't* going to make soup.

His mother filled a pot with water and set it on the stove.

When the water got hot, she threw in some salt.

Then, taking a breath, she screamed into the pot.

"Your turn," she said.
So Horace got on a stool and screamed, too.

His mother screamed louder.

Horace growled and bared his teeth.

The water started to boil.

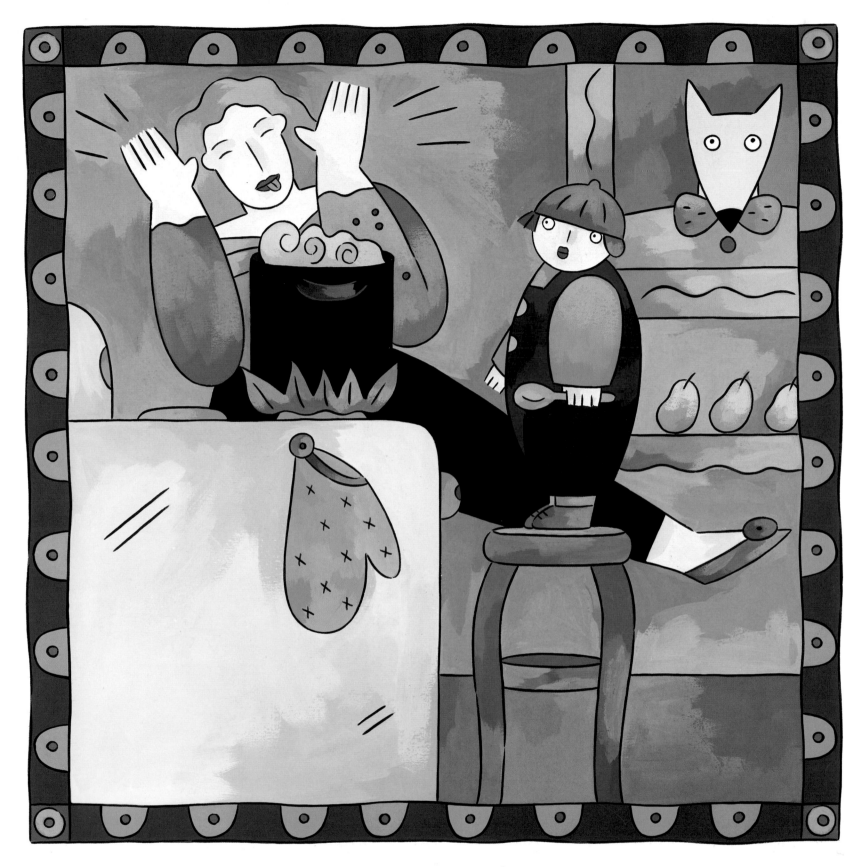

His mother stuck out her tongue.

Horace stuck out his tongue twenty times.

He banged on the pot with a spoon.

He breathed his best dragon breath.

Then he smiled.

His mother smiled, too.

"What's the name of this recipe?" asked Horace.

"Mean Soup," she said.

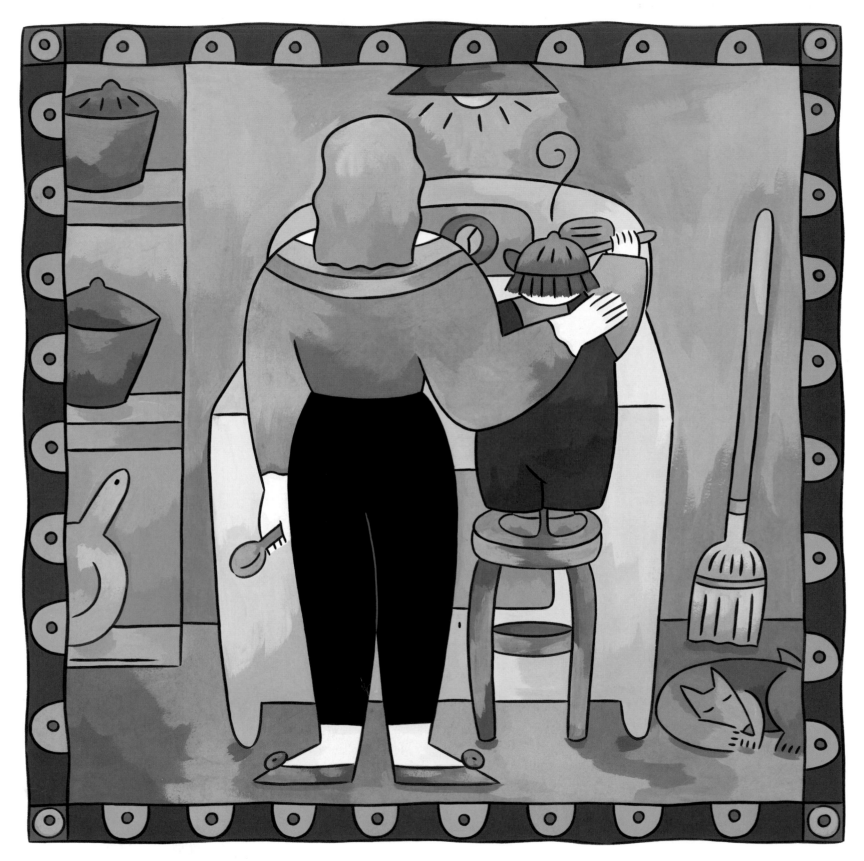

And they stood together, stirring away a bad day.